SPORTS DREAM

"Every good and perfect gift is from above." – James 1:17

I dedicate this book to my husband Jonathan, who pushed and inspired me throughout my journey, and our daughter Harper. It is because of them that I had the confidence to step out and believe that I could. I love you both.

To my parents, Willie, and Roxane Harper. Thank you for being the perfect examples all throughout my life. I am blessed that God created you to be my parents.

To my siblings, Terrell, Willie, Johnny, Sig, Marcus, Matthew, Whitney, and Josh, your stories have become my stories. Thank you for every moment we have shared.

To all my extended family and friends who inspired me to follow my dreams, thank you. I love you.

Qiava Martinez

4

When I was a little girl, dreams floated my way,
Of whom I'd become and the sports I'd play.

Tennis or basketball, my goal was clear,

6

Dreams so big, I wondered if I would persevere.

To be an athlete was greatly in my blood,

8

And for a young girl
what I truly loved.

After school, to the courts, I'd dash.

But my love for the game did not
make me fast.

Though others soared, reaching stars before night,

I knew my journey was its own unique flight.

With every challenge, my spirit grew bolder,

14

Dreams on my shoulders, I became their holder.

College years flew, dreams took a new bend,

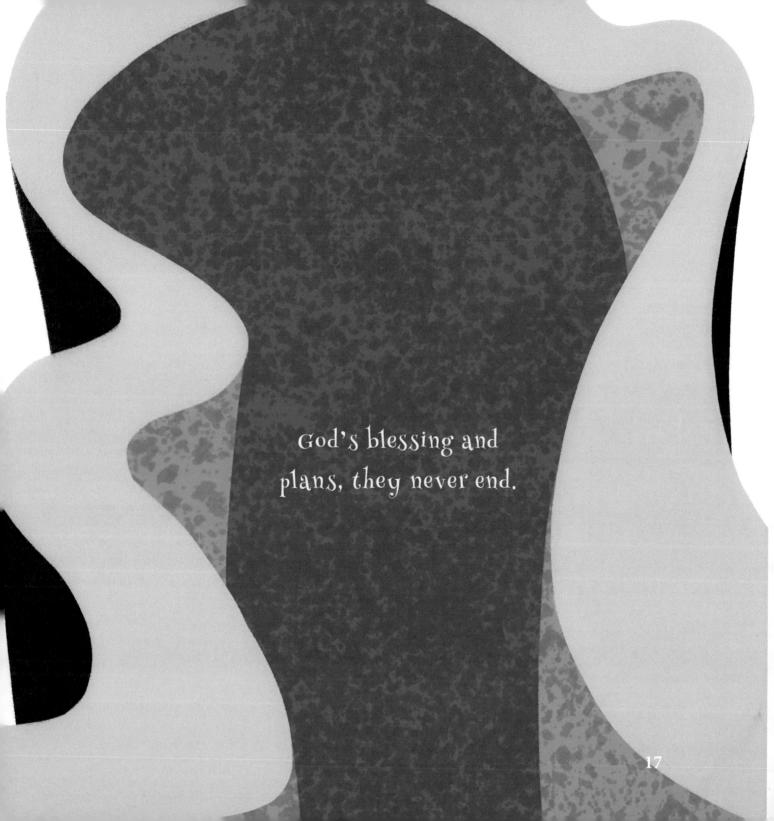

God's blessing and
plans, they never end.

My time arrived, bursting
with sheer glee,

In the vast world of sports, I found where I'd be.

Though not on the field, my aspirations took flight,

In a different direction,
shining just as bright.

Crafting ideas, bigger than dreams of the night.

22

In sports, you can shine off the field,
just as bright.

President, Coach, or even the boss,

Every role is special, no dream is a loss.

EXIT

What does your heart echo?
What's its radiant theme?

Harness that power,
chase that dream.

27

Though some dreams shimmer like distant
stars in the night,
With determination, they come within sight.

Nothing will stop you once you see,
That the dream you have is within
you - just believe!

No matter your start, dreams can soar high,
With grit and belief, you can touch the sky.

Grow, strive, with ambition in your view.
If one path fades, another emerges anew.

Remember these words and shout out loud.

As you walk with confidence with
your shoulders out proud.

I know my dream,
I see it and believe,

34

Nothing can stop me,
I can be whatever I strive to achieve!

Qiava Martinez

Author Sports Dream

In a small town where dreams were often limited by tradition, young Qiava constantly daydreamed about playing sports. From basketball to soccer, there was hardly a game she didn't love. However, her path was laden with obstacles. Many believed that sports weren't for girls, and despite her passion and skills, Qiava often found herself sidelined, watching the boys play.

Determined to stay close to the world of sports, Qiava immersed herself in studying the business side of games. She mastered statistics, team dynamics, and even took an interest in sports marketing.
Her determination and resilience eventually caught the attention of the National Football League.

Rising through the ranks, Qiava became Sr Vice President and Chief Sales Officer (CSO) of an NFL team, breaking ceilings in a traditionally male-dominated arena. And while she might not have become the athlete she'd once envisioned, Qiava discovered that there were multiple ways to be part of the sports world she loved so much.
In "Sports Dream," young readers will learn that even if life doesn't go exactly as planned, with passion and perseverance, dreams can still come true in the most unexpected ways.

Made in the USA
Middletown, DE
24 June 2024

56265661R00022